Unleashing his inner potential is just the beginning. A[d...] choosing how he will use his newfound power.

Determined to defend those who can't defend themselves, Adam turns to four of his bravest friends to join him. When he shares his power with them, he unlocks their inner gifts. His hotheaded best friend, KRASS, becomes RAM MA'AM: Master of Demolition! DUNCAN—a brilliant engineer—becomes MAN-AT-ARMS: Master of Technology! The wise old tiger CRINGER becomes BATTLE CAT: Master of the Wild! Spirited TEELA becomes SORCERESS: Master of Magic! And Adam their leader is HE-MAN: the Master of Power. Together, they are the MASTERS OF THE UNIVERSE!

They've sure got their work cut out for them.

Cackling with monstrous joy, the skull-faced overlord of destruction, SKELETOR, is on the march! Dead set on getting all the cosmos in his bony grasp, if he succeeds, Skeletor will remake everything in existence in his image. Welcome to a grave new world!

It's up to He-Man and his friends to stop them. The Masters of the Universe courageously face off against Skeletor and his Dark Masters.

Will you
join He-Man
and become a Master
of the Universe?
The power is
yours!

CONT

HE-MAN
AND THE MASTERS OF THE UNIVERSE™

HEROES
AND
VILLAINS
GUIDEBOOK

By Rob David and
Melanie Shannon

Scholastic Inc.

ISBN 978-1-338-76085-9
10 9 8 7 6 5 4 3 2   22 23 24 25
Printed in the U.S.A.   40
First printing 2021
Book design by Jeff Shake

YOU HAVE THE POWER!

What if you could turn the ordinary into the extraordinary? Everyone is born with a natural talent or ability. It could be anything, like running fast or solving math problems, playing video games or telling jokes. Whatever your talent is, wouldn't it be cool to get even better at it? What if you could really master it, and transform it into a superpower?

One sixteen-year-old boy named ADAM knows how. On the surface, he's a regular kid. But inside, Adam has the heart of a champion: He wants to help others, and he's got the courage to stand up to bullies. If only he had the power to make a difference.

But he does! When Adam lifts his magic sword and calls upon the ancient powers of the universe, lightning strikes! Suddenly, Adam is transformed into He-Man, the most powerful man in the universe! A power he seeks to *Master*.

ENTS

5: THE WORLD OF ETERNIA

6: VEHICLES

7: THE BATTLE FOR ETERNIA

THE POWER OF GRAYSKULL

At the center of the universe on the radiant planet ETERNIA, the mighty fortress CASTLE GRAYSKULL protects an ancient secret: Behind its stony walls armed with formidable technology and cloaked in layers of magic, hidden deep within the heart of the castle, is the SUPREME POWER CHAMBER.

When Adam and his friends enter this sacred room, they see an enormous column of brilliant crackling energy. This is THE POWER OF GRAYSKULL, the magical nexus of all the ancient powers that created the universe!

1

As our heroes soon discover, the Power of Grayskull has the ability to bring out and amplify the best of you and turn it into a superpower. But not without a Power Weapon!

POWER WEAPONS

POWER WEAPONS are what allow Adam and his friends to connect to the Power of Grayskull. Once upon a time, there was only one Power Weapon: He-Man's Sword of Power, which was created long ago by the legendary King Grayskull himself. But Adam changed all that, when—as He-Man— he used his sword to share the Power of Grayskull with his friends.

He pointed his sword at Teela's staff, Duncan's wrench, Cringer's metal claws, and Krass's trusty old helmet, and transferred the Power of Grayskull into them, turning his friends' belongings into Power Weapons, too. And when that happened, his friends could also call upon the Power of Grayskull!

Now whenever Adam, Teela, Duncan, Cringer, and Krass say the magic words, "BY THE POWER OF GRAYSKULL . . . I HAVE THE POWER," lightning strikes as the Power of Grayskull flows from the castle to their Power Weapons, and then into the kids, turning the kids into Masters of the Universe—magnifying each of their gifts. Their bodies might physically transform (like it does with Adam), or they might gain startling new technological armor (like Duncan does), but for all of them, they now possess new strength.

Adam is figuring out what to call this amazing transformation. Power up? Master up? Upgrade?

One thing's for sure: By the Power of Grayskull, they have the power!

MASTER FORM AND BASE MODE

The Power Weapons that our Heroes wield transform them from their regular, everyday selves—or BASE MODES—into their MASTER FORMS.

Brave, loyal Adam transforms into HE-MAN, the Master of Power. His best friend, Krass, is impulsive and brash, and becomes RAM MA'AM: Master of Demolition! Duncan—a brilliant engineer—becomes MAN-AT-ARMS: Master of Technology! The wise old tiger Cringer becomes BATTLE CAT: Master of the Wild! And spirited Teela becomes SORCERESS: Master of Magic!

In Master Form, they are supercharged warriors, each manifesting the might and magic of an ancient power of the universe! But everyone in Master Form is still themselves underneath. Thoughts, feelings, personality—they're all the

same in Master Form. You always hated mayonnaise? Bulging biceps aren't going to change that.

The first time the kids transformed into their Master Forms, they picked a Master name. Except for Adam! His best friend, Krass, came up with *his* Master name: "He-Man." At first, Adam wasn't sure how he felt about it, "It's like calling myself 'Man-Guy'!" But there are times that the name just seems to fit. He-Man is the perfect name for him.

Transformation into Master Form can last for as long as they are connected to the Power of Grayskull through their weapons. The Masters can power back down into their Base Mode whenever they want, but if their weapon is broken or loses its charge, then they'll be forced to power down.

At first, Teela, Duncan, Krass, and Cringer thought they needed He-Man to charge up their weapons every time they wanted to transform into their Master Forms. But then they realized that once He-Man did it the first time, they could now transform on their own. Like Adam, the other Masters can use their power however—and whenever—they choose.

The kids love their new powers and abilities but don't want to be in their Master Forms all the time. They're still kids, and it's hard to play holo-video games together when they're wearing suits of armor! Besides, they see the Power of Grayskull as a force to use to defend their world, not as something to hold on to all the time for themselves. Adam, Teela, Duncan, Krass—and wise old Cringer, too— aren't just kids at heart. They have the hearts of heroes. That's what makes them the Masters of the Universe!

BASE MODE	MASTER FORM	POWER WEAPON
 Adam	 He-Man, Master of Power	 Sword of Power
 Krass	 Ram Ma'am, Master of Demolition	 Helm of Demolition
 Duncan	 Man-At-Arms, Master of Technology	 Mace of Technology
 Cringer	 Battle Cat, Master of the Wild	Claws of the Wild
 Teela	 Sorceress, Master of Magic	Staff of Magic

POWER WEAPONS: BASE MODES AND MASTER FORMS

Even their weapons have Base Modes and Master Forms, sometimes the differences can be surprising! Duncan's Power Weapon, for example, is a wrench when he's Duncan, but becomes an earth-shattering MACE when he's powered up as Man-At-Arms.

THE PURPOSE OF A MASTER

Adam, Teela, Cringer, Krass, and Duncan are the first Eternians to wield the Power of Grayskull since King Grayskull himself, over a thousand years ago.

They must protect Eternia, her people, and—above all—Castle Grayskull. Should the Power of Grayskull ever be extinguished or captured by the forces of evil, the entire universe—*all* of creation—would fall.

It's a lot of pressure! Especially for Adam and his friends, who are just beginning to learn the ropes. The more they train and the more powers they unlock, the more butt they can kick. But there's more to becoming a Master than slinging around Power Weapons. And under the guidance of Eldress, the ghostly guardian of Castle Grayskull, our heroes must quickly learn THE RULES OF MASTERY!

Now that they have the Power, what are they supposed to do with it?

THE RULES OF MASTERY

Transforming into Master Form is just the beginning of a Master's journey. The title MASTER OF THE UNIVERSE must ultimately be earned—much like earning belts in karate. Each level unlocks new and greater abilities based on the Master's specific Power of the Universe.

IT ALL BEGINS WHEN . . .

. . . the Power Awakens!

Having used a Power Weapon to unlock their natural gift and potential, a new Master must now learn to wield their weapon with purpose and intelligence, honing their newfound skills the way one sharpens a blade. When they do, they'll move up to the next level . . .

. . . Power United!

The Masters must learn to stay focused in the face of fear and come to understand that their greatest power comes from how they are connected to all the other powers—and people—in the universe. The Masters are never as helpless as they may feel, so long as they are together. When they truly understand that, they will move up to the next level . . .

. . . Power Everlasting!

The Master must now overcome their Nemesis—the Dark Master who represents their greatest fear—once and for all. When they do, the Master and their Power will become as one. That is when they will have truly earned the title Master of the Universe.

As Eldress told her young champions, Adam, Teela, Duncan, Krass, and Cringer, when they first began their journey, "Becoming a Master is about learning who you really are, inside and out." The road to Mastery won't be easy for them. Each level is a personal trial. But every time they succeed and level up, they know it.

MASTER STRIKES

When our heroes level up in Mastery, suddenly their eyes glow with golden light, and their weapons unleash a new, spectacular power called a MASTER STRIKE. Or, as the kids just call it, "the gold eyes thing."

They have lots of powers, but their Master Strikes are the greatest of all. He-Man calls the first one he unlocks Lightning Strike—that's when his sword aligns all the heavenly bodies in the universe to call down a strike so cosmically huge, it's capable of flattening mountains.

For Man-At-Arms, it's Speed Build, where time seems to slow down to a crawl as he spins his Power Mace impossibly fast, firing off tendrils of energy that construct amazing pieces of technology in just a fraction of a second.

More and more "Master Strikes" are revealed as Adam and his friends level up. When they learn the lesson of Power United, they gain the ability to activate the Kirbinite in their weapons to combine their Powers into Combo Master Strikes.

For example, when He-Man lets loose his Lightning Strike and Battle Cat lets his Blade Wheels fly, they can fuse their attacks together to create ROLLING THUNDER—a combination of both Master Strikes! Or when Sorceress unleashes her Wings of Zoar just as Man-At-Arms enters Speed Build, they can combine their attacks into GEARS OF ZOAR—where Sorceress's magical falcon multiplies into dozens of devastating falcon drones.

What new Master Strikes will they unlock when they reach full Mastery? Time will tell. They're going to need all the power they can get to fend off Skeletor and his dreaded Dark Masters of the Universe!

Kirbinite is the rarest metal on Eternia, and the only known metal capable of transferring cosmic power. He-Man's Sword of Power is made of Kirbinite, and ever since Duncan used this unique material to mend the other Masters' Power Weapons, all their weapons now contain Kirbinite as well.

MASTER STRIKES:

He-Man	Lightning Strike
Sorceress	Wings of Zoar
Man-At-Arms	Speed Build
Battle Cat	Blade Wheels
Ram Ma'am	unknown

COMPOUND POWERS OF THE UNIVERSE:

He-Man + Battle Cat	Rolling Thunder
Sorceress + Man-At-Arms	Gears of Zoar
He-Man + Sorceress	Lightning Falcon
Battle Cat + Man-At-Arms	Claw-Nado

GRAYSKULL'S SHADOW: THE POWER OF HAVOC

The bright and shimmering Power of Grayskull encompasses all the cosmic forces from the very creation of the universe. But every light has a shadow side, and for the Power of Grayskull, that shadow is HAVOC.

Havoc energy is evil and destructive. It is power that is out of control. It is power without end. It is the flip side of the power that He-Man commands. And just as Adam transforms into He-Man using the Power of Grayskull, his uncle—Prince Keldor—transformed into Skeletor using Havoc. But unlike Adam, Skeletor will never let his power go, never returning to be the man he once was.

Havoc is the source of Skeletor's strength, which he draws upon with his DARK POWER WEAPON, the HAVOC STAFF.

DARK POWER WEAPONS: BASE MODES AND DARK MASTER FORMS

Like the Masters, the Dark Masters' weapons have Base Modes and
Dark Master Forms, and sometimes the differences can be just as
surprising! Skeletor's Havoc Staff, for example, was once a scepter
that Prince Keldor claimed within the halls of Castle Grayskull.
It would revert back to that, if Skeletor would ever revert back
to being Prince Keldor—but that ain't going to happen!

BASE MODE	DARK MASTERS FORM	DARK POWER WEAPON
 Keldor	 Skeletor, Dark Master of Havoc	 Staff of Havoc
 Evelyn	 Evil-Lyn, Dark Master of Witchcraft	Orb of Witchcraft
Kronis	 Trap Jaw, Dark Master of Weaponry	Maw of Weaponry
Rqazz	Beast Man, Dark Master of Beasts	 Lash of Beasts

Now, repeat after him: The sworn duty of every Dark Master is to conquer Eternia and capture Castle Grayskull in the name of the greatest Dark Master of all—SKELETOR!

With his havoc staff, Skeletor creates mighty warriors of his own: DARK MASTERS OF THE UNIVERSE.

Like evil reflections of the heroic Masters of the Universe, Dark Masters follow the same Rules of Mastery as Adam and his friends. Just don't expect any discipline or self-control from this ghoulish gang! Dark Masters train to keep their rage burning at a fever pitch.

But where Adam shared his Power with his friends, Skeletor maintains complete control over his minions. When it's time for battle, he cries out, "Through the purity of Havoc, they have my Power!" At that, Havoc chains erupt from Skeletor's staff, supercharging their DARK POWER WEAPONS and triggering their transformations into terrifying DARK MASTER FORMS.

MASTERS VS. DARK MASTERS

Just like the Power of Grayskull and the Power of Havoc are mirror images of each other, so too are the Masters and the Dark Masters. For each ancient power of the universe there is a dark power that is its shadow reflection. And for every Master, their own Dark Master NEMESIS.

He-Man, Man-At-Arms, Sorceress, and Battle Cat have all met their Nemeses. But as of yet, Ram Ma'am has not. Why that is, she does not know—but it is inevitable that she will. A Nemesis may not be revealed today or even tomorrow, but will appear one day for sure. It is said that whenever a Power Weapon is created, its reflection cannot be far behind.

MASTER / NEMESIS

The Master of Power (He-Man)			The Dark Master of Havoc (Skeletor)
The Master of Magic (Sorceress)			The Dark Master of Witchcraft (Evil-Lyn)
The Master of the Technology (Man-At-Arms)			The Dark Master of Weaponry (Trap Jaw)
The Master of the Wild (Battle Cat)			The Dark Master of Beasts (Beast Man)

ENEMY OR NEMESIS

A Master may have many enemies, but they only have one true Nemesis. A Nemesis represents their personal weaknesses, fears, and flaws; the part of them they must confront and overcome.

ETERNIA'S HEROIC DEFENDERS

Adam's closest allies are Teela, Duncan, Krass, and Cringer, and as He-Man, Sorceress, Man-At-Arms, Ram Ma'am, and Battle Cat, they are a formidable team. More than that, they're orphans who are now a family. And more than THAT, they're teenagers— superpowered teenagers! Battles for the remote control can end in needing a new roof on Castle Grayskull. (As the adult in the room, Cringer takes no responsibility.) Under the watchful eye of Eldress, these heroes embark on the most epic of adventures. When they raise their Power Weapons and call upon the Power of Grayskull, they become THE MASTERS OF THE UNIVERSE!

ADAM

Sixteen-year-old Adam grew up in Eternia's mountain regions in the Tiger Tribe—a close-knit community of humans and talking green tigers. These great cats have been taking in strays—any men, women, and children in need of a home—for eons. They discovered Adam when he was just six years old, all alone and lost in the woods, and raised him like one of their own.

Ever adventurous, Adam spent his days as an assistant cat tracker. He loved his job, exploring the rocky terrain with the energetic

Growing up, Adam had no idea that he was actually the Prince of Eternia, son of King Randor, who rules from the capital city of Eternos. And Skeletor? That's Adam's uncle, Prince Keldor. When Adam was six, Keldor attempted to overthrow King Randor and steal the Power of Grayskull, using Adam as a hostage. Ultimately, that day, to protect young Adam from Keldor—and the looming danger of Skeletor, Eldress hid him among the Tiger Tribe. Adam grew up not knowing who he really was or where he really came from, and his father, King Randor, never knew what happened to his son. This was necessary so that Adam could grow up to become the man who would one day take down Skeletor.

furballs. His best friends in the tribe? Krass, who's kinda like his kid sister, and the old cat known affectionately as Cringer, who's the closest thing to a father Adam's ever had.

Adam didn't mind having such a low-ranking position in the tribe. He never wanted power or responsibility. But all that changed when Skeletor and his cronies appeared to threaten Eternia. In that moment, Adam made the most startling discovery: He was not an orphan, but the lost Prince of Eternia! The one person destined to wield a blade powerful enough to save Eternia and protect Castle Grayskull—the SWORD OF POWER!

Adam gripped the Sword of Power, and—accompanied by Krass and

Cringer—left the Tiger Tribe behind to stop them. He knew he had to do what's right and fight the evil—no matter how frightening the challenge. Being a champion is about defending people who can't defend themselves. That's the *strength* the Power of Grayskull saw in Adam—the inner strength worthy of the Sword of Power.

He held the sword aloft and gave a shout: "By the Power of Grayskull, I have the Power!" And with that, Adam transformed into the mighty He-Man!

HE-MAN

Gifted with bone-shattering strength! Stamina so great he can take on entire armies! Sword strikes so powerful they can cleave mountains in two! HE-MAN is the MASTER OF POWER!

Inside, he's still Adam, but now he has mighty rippling muscles. He-Man's incredible strength surpasses that of anyone on Eternia. He is quicker than most and difficult to harm.

His sword is almost indestructible and can cut through most materials. It's also able to deflect energy and magic when used to shield attacks. He-Man can rip mighty trees from the earth, hold back avalanches, and launch evil beasts into the stratosphere.

He-Man's power is represented by the glowing magical tattoos on his upper body: his sigil, which first appeared on those bulging biceps the first time he called upon the Power of Grayskull. Now, whenever He-Man powers up to deliver the mightiest of moves, those tats glow for all the world to see.

His most powerful moves are his Master Strikes. That's when he aligns himself with the full power of the universe.

But his most amazing ability is that his sword has the power to transform others into Masters of the Universe, as demonstrated when Adam shared the power with his friends Teela, Krass, Duncan, and Cringer. Or perhaps that doesn't say as much about the sword as it does about Adam. The sword is the key to the castle and all its power, and Adam is the one worthy to wield it because he doesn't keep the power all for himself.

NAME—BASE MODE: Adam

NAME—MASTER FORM: He-Man

TITLE: Master of Power

POWER WEAPON: Sword of Power

MASTER STRIKE: Lightning Strike

POWER SYMBOL:

POWER COLOR:

NEMESIS: Skeletor, Dark Master of Havoc

CRINGER

The eldest of the wild talking cats of the Tiger Tribe, Cringer is sage and wise but still up for adventure. In fact, it was Cringer who found six-year-old Adam lost and confused in the jungle all those years ago. From that day on, the old cat watched over Adam.

Today, the two have a special bond. Cringer's always there to offer Adam advice and help him out of sticky situations. To Adam, Cringer is part father, part friend. Cringer would stand by Adam no matter what.

He was once the most ferocious wild cat there was, until he was captured

Cringer has four nephews, all bright and wildly energetic tiger cubs: Cormac, Cassius, Connor, and little Cadum. All the kids in the tribe call Cadum "Kitty." As the youngest and most energetic of the bunch, Kitty seems to have a particular knack for getting into trouble. But given enough time, this sprightly cub could grow up to be the next Master of the Wild!

by a hunter named Rqazz. Rqazz put animals in fighting pits, and that's where he sent Cringer. But Cringer refused to fight. As punishment, Rqazz stole Cringer's claws as a trophy and gave the defiant tiger the nickname Cringer as an insult. But Cringer escaped and chose to own the name as a sign of pride. There's nothing wrong with choosing your battles and only fighting for what's right. And kicking Skeletor's bony butt is the greatest right there is! Especially after Skeletor makes Rqazz the Dark Master, Beast Man.

But what use is a tiger without his claws? Fortunately, Duncan was able to make artificial claws for Cringer, and Adam supercharged them to become Cringer's power weapon—Power Claws of the Wild! Now Cringer can transform into the ferocious Battle Cat—Master of the Wild!

BATTLE CAT

As Battle Cat, Cringer is fast, wild, and empowered—thirsty for victory and justice. Clad in crimson armor, he's now bigger than a horse—easily big enough for He-Man to ride into battle. Cringer is now Master of all that is untamable in the universe.

NAME—BASE MODE: Cringer

NAME—MASTER FORM: Battle Cat

TITLE: Master of the Wild

POWER WEAPON: Claws of the Wild

MASTER STRIKE: Blade Wheels

POWER SYMBOL:

POWER COLOR:

NEMESIS: Beast Man,
Dark Master of Beasts

KRASS

Krass grew up in the Tiger Tribe with Adam. At just fifteen, Krass is pretty much a younger sister to Adam. She's got a big heart, particularly for her Tiger Tribe family, and she's spirited.

But if anything sets her off, watch out! Krass's solution to any problem is to headbutt first, think later. That's why Adam calls her Rammy. Busting up a problem usually helps clear her head. And once she's done, she's *done*. Don't expect her to clean up any messes, or even think of putting back together whatever she's just demolished. Krass will be bouncing off to something new before the wreckage has even hit the ground.

She's fearless and fun but can also be overconfident—believing that things will turn out her way, whether or not there's evidence to back it up. But underneath Krass's stubborn exterior is a sweet side.

Krass was adopted by the Tiger Tribe as a child, after her parents' ship crash-landed in the jungle. Krass was the only survivor, thanks to her dad's oversized helmet, which she was wearing at the time. The helmet kept her alive, but if it weren't for the tribe, she might never have recovered. The Tiger Tribe means everything to her, and she couldn't wait to get her STRIPES—the tribe's official tattoo that says you're family.

The fact that Adam never chose to get those stripes bothers Krass to no end and has been the subject of countless arguments between the two. While she's happy to defend the universe from Adam's new digs at Castle Grayskull, Krass never forgets where they came from and worries they may have strayed too far from their tribal roots.

When Adam charged Krass's helmet with the Power of Grayskull, it became her Power Weapon: the Helm of Demolition. Now Krass uses it to transform into Ram Ma'am, Master of Demolition!

RAM MA'AM

Crusted into the front of Krass's helmet is a special gem that won't ever come loose. In the helmet's Master Form, that gem enlarges to become a formidable battering ram filled with the energy of Demolition.

As Ram Ma'am, her powered-up helmet ignites her rocket-fueled boots, blasting her off into RAM BALL action—bouncing her around at breakneck speeds, crushing anything in her path with her head. She's a human super-ball battering ram. Ram Ma'am's helmet even absorbs the force of impact when she hits an object, so it doesn't hurt or slow her down one bit—but instead converts the impact into more kinetic energy and speed!

The only thing that can slow her down are energy bands that fire from her armor, latching on to the nearest large object and yanking her back. But who wants to slow down? Not Ram Ma'am! She prefers to use these bands to slingshot herself even faster. Ram Ma'am is a force of demolition!

NAME—BASE MODE: Krass

NAME—MASTER FORM: Ram Ma'am

TITLE: Master of Demolition

POWER WEAPON: Helm of Demolition

MASTER STRIKE: Unknown

POWER SYMBOL:

POWER COLOR:

NEMESIS: Unknown

TEELA

For as long as Teela can remember, she's been on her own—growing up alone on the streets of Eternos. As a little girl she was taken in by Man-E-Faces, the self-proclaimed King of the Lower Wards. He gave her shelter and taught her how to survive on the streets, mainly by fighting and thieving—especially if it's for pay. Now sixteen, Teela is street smart: resourceful, fiercely independent, and spirited. She has a good habit of saying what she thinks, and she's a fighter. Whatever trouble her mouth gets her into, her hand-to-hand combat skills can usually get her out of it.

Teela's also a natural-born witch. Without knowing how or why, she's just always had the ability to perform small acts of hand magic. At first it was simple things, like summoning a flickering blue flame in the palm of her hand to light her way in dim back alleys. Or drawing in midair with just the tip of her finger, creating sparkling blue images of castles, great winged birds, and jewel-like planets to keep her company in the dark of night.

It's that quick-witted and clever attitude, along with Teela's desire to keep innocent bystanders out of harm's way, that almost instantly made her one of Adam's closest friends. When Adam is messing up, Teela is the first to let him know.

Teela knows little of her past. But even growing up, she felt something calling to her beyond Eternos. Literally.

Along with her magic powers, she's always been haunted by a mysterious voice and visions of Castle Grayskull. She's done anything she could to follow them—sensing they would lead her to answers about who she really is. Evelyn, knowing this, would hire the young Teela to seek out and bring to her any artifacts of Grayskull Teela could find. But when Teela found the Sword of Power, the mysterious voice told her not to deliver it to Evelyn, but instead to deliver it to the "Champion," Adam. And she did.

Since meeting Adam, she's discovered that the mysterious voice is Eldress—the spirit guardian and former Sorceress of Castle Grayskull. Feeling a special kinship to Eldress, Teela took up her former weapon: a falcon staff. Adam empowered the staff to allow Teela to transform into the *next* Sorceress of Grayskull, the Master of Magic.

SORCERESS

As Sorceress, Teela is cloaked in falcon garb glowing with the magic of the cosmos, and her POWER STAFF gives her tremendous mystical powers. Now she no longer needs to use her hands to cast magic, but with a single thought, Sorceress

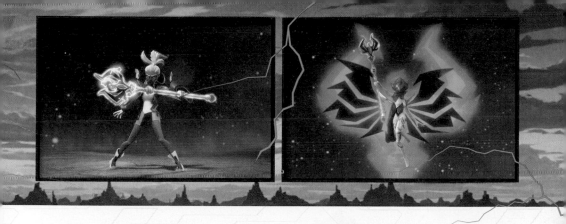

can summon, conjure, transfigure, and more. Her cosmic falcon wings allow her to fly and teleport herself and others. With her Master Strike—Wings of Zoar—Sorceress can summon the great bird of the cosmos, the magical falcon ZOAR, that swoops through a battlefield to sweep away all foes.

But her magic is far from foolproof; Teela is still a sorceress in training. The Power Staff allows her to focus and amplify her magic, but she is still learning to master it. If she isn't careful, she could accidentally teleport her friends into a volcano!

Even so, out of all the Masters, Teela is the most in tune with Castle Grayskull. It feels like home to her, and she's not sure exactly why. What is her special connection with Eldress? Where does she truly come from? Why has the voice of Eldress spoken to her for as long as she can remember?

It will take time for Teela to learn the answers, but she'll have the wisdom of the ages if she can. Until then, she's just a bold and adventurous sixteen-year-old kid.

NAME—BASE MODE: Teela

NAME—MASTER FORM: Sorceress

TITLE: Master of Magic

POWER WEAPON: Staff of Magic

MASTER STRIKE: Wings of Zoar

POWER SYMBOL:

POWER COLOR:

NEMESIS: Evil-Lyn, Dark Master of Witchcraft

DUNCAN

An innovative apprentice weapons maker, Duncan was once on the side of the baddies. This young man chose to join Adam on account of his own fierce desire to create rather than destroy. He wields a Power Mace that transforms him into the Master of Technology.

Duncan is seventeen years old and naturally wired for science and logic. With the mathematically creative mind of an engineer, he easily sees

how everything fits together. He has an uncanny ability to detect the flaw in any system, and the brilliance not only to repair it but also to improve it.

While Duncan is a Master of the Universe, he didn't exactly start off with the good guys.

Duncan grew up in the Eternos orphanage until he became the ward and apprentice of Kronis—the weapons master and man-at-arms to King Randor, until he tried to overthrow the king. Kronis has been a criminal on the run ever since, and the only reason he kept Duncan around was to force the kid to help him build all sorts of horrible weapons for crime.

Though Duncan learned a lot of tricks and tech skills from Kronis, he couldn't bear the idea of using his creations for evil. Because of this, Duncan ultimately developed the courage to rebel against the only father he had ever known, and joined up with Adam to protect Eternia. Now he uses his skills to create weapons, gadgets, and gear for him and his friends to use against Kronis, and against Kronis's new boss, Skeletor!

Although brilliant, Duncan is insecure, more likely to downplay his abilities than not. His biggest insecurity? That he's really nothing more than an invention of Kronis's. But Duncan makes up for it with humor and joy, and his open-minded approach helps him come up with practical solutions to even the most difficult situations.

Since Adam supercharged Duncan's wrench, it transforms into a Power Mace, making Duncan Man-At-Arms, Master of Technology!

MAN-AT-ARMS

As Man-At-Arms, Duncan becomes fitted with high-tech armor. His Power Mace can generate a force field, launch drones, fire missiles, and more. It's even great for smashing things to pieces. And with his Master Strike—Speed Build—he can use his mace to then reconnect those pieces into any technological weapon, device, or vehicle he can imagine. Laser turrets! Attak Traks! Mustache trimmers! And more!

But the conflict between Duncan and Kronis isn't over yet. Though Duncan is empowered as Man-At-Arms, Kronis has become the dreaded Trap Jaw, Dark Master of Weaponry, Skeletor's chief inventor of horrifying tech. Now their conflict is a full-blown arms race between good and evil!

NAME—BASE MODE: Duncan

NAME—MASTER FORM: Man-At-Arms

TITLE: Master of Technology

POWER WEAPON: Mace of Technology

MASTER STRIKE: Speed Build

POWER SYMBOL:

POWER COLOR:

NEMESIS: Trap Jaw, Dark Master of Weaponry

ORK-0

Out of all of Duncan's creations, his most ambitious (and totally accidental) is this little magical robot.

Duncan only meant to repair one of King Randor's Rk-0 hover combat droids. This particular one had taken a hit in battle that was intended for Man-At-Arms, and Duncan felt it was the least he could do to thank the little bot. But a funny thing happened on the way to fixing it: drawing on spare parts he'd found in Castle Grayskull's archives, Duncan unintentionally installed an ancient Trollan data disc into the Rk-0 unit's mainframe. When the droid came back online, it no longer knew anything about combat; instead, it—he—was convinced he was Orko, the greatest Trollan wizard of all!

Now calling himself Ork-0, every time this scrambled droid tries to cast a spell, it backfires spectacularly . . . usually on Man-At-Arms, which drives Duncan crazy. Robots and magic just don't mix! Especially when he's not using magic but rather contorting his own robot abilities past all safety protocols. But Ork-0 never gives up on his dream to be the greatest wizard of all time. Witnessing this determination, Duncan can't bring himself to reboot the little bot. Plus, Duncan and the Masters have grown to love Ork-0, and he's even saved their lives more than once.

Maybe one day Ork-0 will also become a Master. Of Magic? Not likely. More like . . . the Master of Disaster! At least that's what Duncan lovingly calls him.

ELDRESS (THE ELDER SORCERESS OF GRAYSKULL)

For centuries, this wise woman of mystery has guarded Castle Grayskull's power in her role as the Sorceress of Grayskull. Though she was once flesh and blood, her true origin is a secret she guards as closely as the Power she's sworn to protect.

Years ago, she gave her life to stop Prince Keldor. Now he's returned as the Dark Master, Skeletor, and she is a spirit who remains in Castle Grayskull. She may not be living, but she still fights Skeletor by mentoring Adam and his friends.

She's warm, kind, and wise, but she only tells our heroes just enough to help them along the way; some answers they need to discover on their own. Perhaps her greatest secret of all, besides the location of Grayskull's bathroom? The truth behind her special connection with Teela.

KING RANDOR

Adam's father, King Randor, rules Eternos—the capital city of Eternia. Heavy is the head that wears the crown, and Randor's bears the added weight of heartache. After all, for ten years he believed he'd lost his older brother and his only son forever. Now he knows his brother is alive, but not only was Keldor responsible for Adam's disappearance, he's corrupted himself and is threatening the entire realm as Skeletor.

Even so, these days the king is smiling once again. Why? Because Adam is alive! And just in time for the teenage years. As happy as they are to be back in each other's lives, Adam and the King don't always see eye to eye.

THE LEGEND OF KING GRAYSKULL

While Adam wields the Sword of Power, it was his ancestor King Grayskull who forged the sword and was the first Master of the Universe. His strength increased a thousandfold, and legend says that with his sword he destroyed the Snake Men Empire during the Great War.

All the people of Eternia—on land, sky, and sea—loved Grayskull, and under his rule they were united. But when he died, that unity fell apart. The realm fractured into three separate kingdoms: Eternos of the land, Avion of the sky, and Leviathae of the sea.

Their biggest disagreement? That Adam wields the Sword of Power.

The Power of Grayskull has been a secret held close by Kings of Eternos for a millennium—since the time of the greatest king of all, KING GRAYSKULL. The stories say that a thousand years ago, King Grayskull used his Sword of Power to defeat the evil SNAKE MEN. No one else was as strong of spirit and pure of heart to wield this Power, and when King Grayskull died, his descendants locked up Castle Grayskull and the Sword of Power and moved the throne to the city of Eternos. For King Randor, nothing is more important than keeping Castle Grayskull and the Sword of Power a secret and off-limits to everyone.

That is, until he saw his son, Adam, as He-Man, wield the Power of Grayskull to defend the realm against Skeletor. He's proud of Adam but still worries about his son. And he's certainly not sure how he feels about Adam sharing the Power with his friends—not to mention now that the kids have moved into Castle Grayskull. Word is they're bunking in the castle's archives. Next thing you know, they'll turn the Meditation Pool into a hot tub.

Randor longs for the day that Adam will take on his rightful role as Prince and move into Eternos Palace to sit in the chair at Randor's right hand. Adam is glad to know his dad, and they're growing closer, but considering Adam only just found out he's a prince, he's not ready to take that seat just yet.

ETERNOS MILITARY

As the good king of Eternos, Randor is dedicated to defending Castle Grayskull and all his people from harm. Though he and Adam may have their arguments, Randor upholds his duty by helping He-Man and the Masters in the fight against Skeletor, most often by sending in the Eternos Military.

GENERAL DOLOS

The leader of the Eternos military, and King Randor's most trusted friend and strategist.

TUVAR AND BADDRAH

Two average soldiers in the Royal Palace Guard, these guys always seem to be in the wrong place at the wrong time . . . or is it the wrong place at the right time? Don't worry, they're still trying to figure this one out, too.

THE RED LEGION

General Dolos's elite special forces of the most highly trained and well-armed soldiers of Eternos. They're known for their crimson ships. If you're a bad guy and you hear the sonic booms of their engines approaching, it would be best to flee.

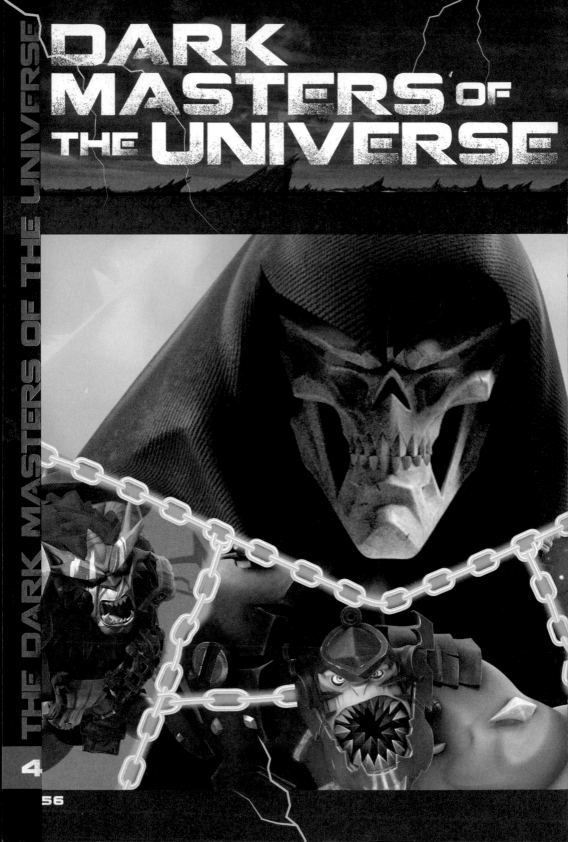

DARK MASTERS OF THE UNIVERSE

THE SCOURGE OF ETERNIA

In his headquarters of SNAKE MOUNTAIN, Skeletor strikes the ground with his staff, injecting the earth with his Dark Havoc Power, creating an unnatural fiery pit. Here, to confront He-Man and his heroic Masters, he forges new Dark Power Weapons to assemble his own Masters of the Universe—Dark Masters!

But unlike He-Man, Skeletor isn't truly sharing his power. The weapons of the Dark Masters are more like leashes, thanks to the Kirbinite Skeletor infused into them. Now, with his Havoc Staff, Skeletor can turn their power on and off. He can even turn his Dark Masters into puppets if they dare defy him.

KELDOR

Once upon a time, Skeletor was Keldor, the Prince of Eternos. But he was never content to be only a prince. He wanted to be the king, and he saw the Power of Grayskull as the surest way to steal the throne from his brother, King Randor.

Keldor kidnapped Randor's six-year-old son, Adam, as a hostage and stormed his way to the Jawbridge of Castle Grayskull. There, he demanded that Eldress let him inside, or he would end young Adam's life.

Seeing no choice, Eldress lowered the Jawbridge. At last, Keldor

would take the Power of Grayskull for himself!

But once inside, Keldor had his own choice to make. Eldress presented him with two totems of Grayskull: a sword and a scepter, saying that proper use of the Power requires the selection of a totem for mastery of oneself. He must choose wisely.

Keldor chose the scepter, seeing it as the totem of a true ruler, such as himself.

But he chose poorly; the Power of Grayskull is a good judge of character. When Keldor thrust the scepter into the heart of its energy—to claim and master it—

the Power of Grayskull deemed him unworthy. The energy reacted violently, coursing dark Havoc magic through him, *cursing him*, turning Keldor's inner darkness outward.

Eldress was ultimately able to cast Keldor out that day and to hide Adam in the safety of the Tiger Tribe, but the battle came at the cost of her own life.

Ten years later, Keldor has returned! No longer does he see himself as cursed by Havoc but rather *blessed* by it. Keldor allowed Havoc to fully transform him forever into the skull-faced demon, SKELETOR. To him, the Power of Grayskull is a lie, and Havoc is superior.

SKELETOR

Skeletor *enjoys* his Dark Power of Havoc, the opposite of the power that He-Man commands. Similar to Keldor himself, his scepter transformed via this magic to become a staff capped by a terrifying ram skull: the HAVOC STAFF.

SKELETOR PLANS TO:

1 CONQUER ETERNIA

2 ENSLAVE ITS PEOPLE

3 STEAL ITS RESOURCES

4 CAPTURE CASTLE GRAYSKULL

5 FINISH HIS AUTOBIOGRAPHY

IT'S ONE SERIOUSLY WICKED BUCKET LIST.

With his Havoc Staff, Skeletor becomes the pumped-up, supercharged, skull-faced villain who now strikes fear in the hearts of all: the Dark Master of Havoc! With bone-chilling strength! Staff strikes so terrible they rip realms apart! And death breath so overpowering it sends his enemies flying.

Skeletor hates Adam and Adam's alter ego, He-Man. His jealousy knows no bounds. He resents the very sight of He-Man and his Sword of Power. Grayskull has deemed this *boy* to be more worthy than Keldor? BAH!

Skeletor's even more shocked that He-Man decides to share his power with his friends, entrusting them with Power Weapons, too. Double BAH! Power shared is wasted, according to Skeletor; it must be controlled by the vision and strength of one person!

If you haven't noticed, Skeletor is obsessed with power; consumed with acquiring more and fearful of losing it. Where Adam is willing to share power, Skeletor is unable to ever let it go—literally! Even when the volatile power of his Havoc eats away the flesh of his arm, leaving nothing but a bony grip!

Cold and calculating, Skeletor is extremely intelligent, manipulative, and not to be underestimated. He has an evil streak and gets a real kick out of teasing and torturing others—including his very own minions.

While he taunts and intimidates with joy and cutting wit, he does have underlying insecurities about losing the respect of his troops.

His overinflated self-importance means he's won't lift a finger if he can get a minion to do something for him instead. But these weaknesses aside, make no mistake: Skeletor is a strong warrior who loves bringing down the final death blow.

As Dark Master of Havoc, Skeletor's staff can shatter most anything and lends him enhanced strength. He

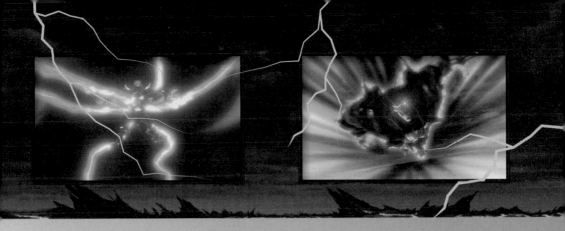

can release powerful shockwaves of Havoc energy, blasting all enemies back. He can drain the life force from creatures and people, turning them to stone. He can even manipulate his Havoc to control the minds of others.

His most powerful move is his Dark Master Strike, called Havoc Strike. That's when Skeletor plunges into the depths of Havoc to emerge with a blow that bring the Masters to their knees.

Unlike all the other Masters, Skeletor is the only one who stays in his Dark Master Mode all the time. For one thing, he will never ever relinquish one drop of his power. Ever. And also, he can't! "Skeletor" (his Master Form) is a curse, the inner darkness of Prince Keldor (his Base Mode) turned outward. There is no going back.

Good! Skeletor prefers it that way. He loves being the skull-faced, demonic Dark Master of Havoc!

- **NAME—BASE MODE:** Keldor
- **NAME—DARK MASTER FORM:** Skeletor
- **TITLE:** Dark Master of Havoc
- **DARK POWER WEAPON:** Staff of Havoc
- **DARK MASTER STRIKE:** Havoc Strike
- **POWER SYMBOL:**
- **POWER COLOR:**
- **NEMESIS:** He-Man, Master of Power

EVELYN

A talented "word witch" who casts spells by speaking, Evelyn once held the coveted title of King Randor's court magician. But she was obsessed with the legends of the Power of Grayskull. Finding the castle and accessing its power was all she could think about, and she grew frustrated by Randor's refusal to even discuss the subject. She sought someone bold enough to seize Grayskull's power . . . someone just like Prince Keldor.

Evelyn sided with Keldor in his coup against Randor—an uprising that ended in failure and resulted in Randor banishing Evelyn from Eternos. But her desire for the power could not be suppressed. She spent the next ten years on a mad search for any and all Grayskull artifacts she could find, including Castle Grayskull itself. She's jealous of Teela, whom Evelyn believes has lucked into her role as the new Sorceress of Grayskull.

Now Evelyn serves Prince Keldor once again, this time as his right hand in his new form as Skeletor. To Evelyn's great delight, the Dark Master of Havoc has granted her a Dark Power Orb infused with his power, capable of transforming her into Evil-Lyn, the Dark Master of Witchcraft!

EVIL-LYN

Where Evelyn must speak her spells into action, Evil-Lyn has no such limitations. Her magic magnified a thousandfold, her power knows no bounds— except for Skeletor, who can turn it off with a snap of his bony fingers.

Evil-Lyn is both Skeletor's greatest ally and worst enemy. The most talented and intelligent of all the Dark Masters, her new Havoc-based magic makes her second only to Skeletor, a fact that immensely frustrates her. While she's

aligned with Skeletor's aims, she's not content to play second best. Secretly, she plots to bump him off, take over, and rule Eternia herself. She often recruits other spies, mercenaries, and even other Dark Masters for her schemes, and delights in bossing them around. But inevitably, after each rebellious outburst or failed coup, Evil-Lyn falls back under Skeletor's command. Perhaps, one day, that will change.

Her Dark Power Weapon is a long staff topped by a crystal orb. With it, she wields great power over the supernatural. As the Dark Master of Witchcraft, Evil-Lyn can summon, conjure, and transfigure. With her Dark Master Strike— Wings of Horokoth—Evil-Lyn can summon the winged magical creature HOROKOTH, a terrifying cosmic bat that screeches across the battlefield to destroy all foes.

NAME—BASE MODE: Evelyn

NAME—DARK MASTER FORM: Evil-Lyn

TITLE: Dark Master of Witchcraft

DARK POWER WEAPON: Orb of Witchcraft

DARK MASTER STRIKE: Wings of Horokoth

POWER SYMBOL:

POWER COLOR:

NEMESIS: Sorceress, Master of Magic

KRONIS

Kronis once served King Randor as the royal man-at-arms, until—along with his partner in crime, Evelyn—he sided with Prince Keldor in his fateful coup to overtake the throne. When their takeover failed, and Keldor and Adam were both presumed to be dead, Kronis and Evelyn were both stripped of their titles and banished from the kingdom.

For ten years, Kronis and Evelyn were left to their own evil plans; Kronis aided Evelyn in her search for Castle Grayskull and the incredible promise of power held inside. And now that Keldor has returned as Skeletor, this time knowing the exact location of Castle Grayskull—Kronis and Evelyn are right back at his side and serving evil. After all these years, the gang is back together again!

Kronis is a skilled mechanic and inventor—a master of traps and weaponry—a trade he passed on to his apprentice, Duncan. When Duncan separated from Kronis (on account of that whole "serving evil" thing), the two battled, leaving Kronis with a broken jaw. But Kronis constructed himself a metal brace, which Skeletor has infused with Havoc, transforming it into a Dark Power Weapon: the Maw of Weaponry that transforms Kronis into Trap Jaw, Dark Master of Weaponry!

TRAP JAW

Trap Jaw is a monster of muscle and mechanical might, with a robotic right arm that can pulverize his enemies. But his true strength comes from his Dark Power Weapon: a cybernetic jaw filled with a vortex of whirling blades. This Maw of Weaponry can distend to devour anything, including machinery.

When Trap Jaw unleashes his Dark Power Strike—Mecha-Maw—his jaw sucks in and shreds metal, gears, and engines into bits that he eats, then fuses back together and spits out through his mechanized right arm in the form of all-new deadly weapons: laser chain saws, missile launchers, destructo-drones, and more!

Trap Jaw also invents tools and vehicles of destruction for Skeletor and his fellow Dark Masters. He's a true bully who enjoys watching his inventions inflict pain—yet another reason his former apprentice Duncan is glad to have joined up with Adam. Trap Jaw, however, has a hard time accepting Duncan's decision, and secretly believes that one day he'll return to serve again at his master's side. After all, Duncan is his greatest "invention."

NAME—BASE MODE: Kronis

NAME—DARK MASTER FORM: Trap Jaw

TITLE: Dark Master of Weaponry

DARK POWER WEAPON: Maw of Weaponry

DARK MASTER STRIKE: Mecha-Maw

POWER SYMBOL:

POWER COLOR:

NEMESIS: Man-At-Arms, Master of Technology

RQAZZ

Originally from a jungle race of savage bestial-human hybrids called Beastopoids—fierce rivals of the Tiger Tribe—Rqazz was born the runt of his litter. But though smaller in size than his siblings, inside he was the most ferocious of all, and he made up for his size with an evil streak.

A natural hunter, Rqazz learned early on that he wasn't going to be happy by merely defeating his prey. Soon he began capturing the creatures of the jungle and putting them in his fighting pits, forcing them to battle against one another for his amusement. Cringer of the Tiger Tribe was one of his victims. And though Cringer eventually escaped, Rqazz still wears his claws as a trophy.

Rqazz serves Skeletor now, who fashioned for him a sinister Dark Power Weapon: the Lash of Beasts, allowing Rqazz to fully unleash his cruelty as Beast Man, Dark Master of Beasts!

BEAST MAN

Overlord of all beasts and monsters, Beast Man has heightened senses, making it almost impossible to sneak up on him or catch him unaware. His temper is violent and ferocious, and he's always looking for an excuse to crack his whip.

Like the dark primal power at his command, Beast Man can never truly be tamed. Though loyal to Skeletor, Beast Man has difficulty following orders. Not that he seeks power, but rather he's a creature of instinct, so he has a hard time following through, especially if the plans are complicated.

His Dark Master Strike is Necro Echo. With a crack of his whip, Beast Man summons a savage creature to attack his foes, one of three vicious, spectral reincarnations of his most prized prey, each represented by a skull worn on his chest: a tiger, a vulture, and a giant spider.

Beast Man's Havoc-powered lash is so precious to him that he is fiercely grateful and loves it when Skeletor calls him "Beastie-my-Bestie." He would sleep at the foot of Skeletor's bed if he'd let him (he doesn't). Rqazz was always a beast inside; now Skeletor has set that beast free as the Beast Man.

🐾 **NAME—BASE MODE:** Rqazz

🐾 **NAME—DARK MASTER FORM:** Beast Man

🐾 **TITLE:** Dark Master of Beasts

🐾 **DARK POWER WEAPON:** Lash of Beasts

🐾 **DARK MASTER STRIKE:** Necro Echo

🐾 **POWER SYMBOL:**

🐾 **POWER COLOR:**

🐾 **NEMESIS:** Battle Cat, Master of the Wild

MAP OF ETERNIA

PLANET ETERNIA

Planet Eternia is the first planet of creation located in the heart of the universe, the nexus of all things: space, time, and the very fabric of the cosmos.

Everything that ever was or will be flows through this magical first world. You can see this in the mixture of cultures, creatures, and civilizations on Eternia: robots, wizards, pirates, warriors, dragons, fighter planes, monsters—Eternia is the nexus of all!

Eternia is bursting with exotic life-forms of all types and countless epic landscapes to match, from fantastic beasts that prowl the land (Ecto-Eels, Basilisks, and more!) to civilized species, like: the Pelleezeans—skunk-like humanoids; the Widgets—a race of dwarfs; Andreenids—a colony of bee-people; the Mossmen—a race of plant-people; and *dozens* more.

Eternia's landscapes are vast and full of life. It's a hopeful world but not for the faint of heart. Some areas are highly technological, and wherever it is being used, the technology is clean,

green, and used with respect for the land. There are also elements that are magical. Pillars of light glow from naturally formed snow chimneys. Giant frozen bubbles hang below the water's surface. A maze of crystal caves form an underground tunnel network. Huge stones "sail" across the lands like a slow-moving herd of elephants. Fairy circles dance through the air in blue forests.

The planet is divided into three realms: the land, the sky, and the sea. King Randor rules over the land from his throne in the city of Eternos. King Stratos guards over the skylands from his perch in the clouds of Avion. King Mer-Man rules Eternia's oceans from the depths of Leviathae.

Despite all their differences, the peoples of Eternia try their best to live side by side in peaceful harmony with their surroundings and one another. There have, however, been tensions between the three kingdoms ever since the end of the Great War and the passing of King Grayskull a thousand years ago. Fortunately, the realms have not yet gone to war.

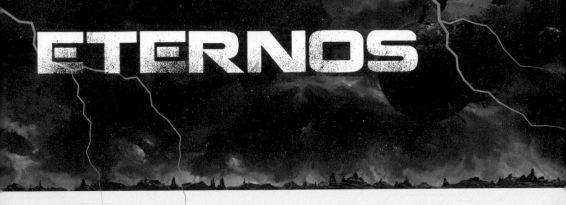

ETERNOS

ternos is the capital of planet Eternia's lands—a large, soaring city surrounded by a green valley. Its sparkling skyscrapers and towers encircle the central palace of Randor. The king's symbol, a golden gryphon, tops the palace.

It's a city of light, with a glow that can be seen from light-years away. Rather than stretching across the horizon, the cityscape of Eternos soars into the sky, its Upper Ward neighborhoods built on floating levels that defy gravity. And there's even more to the city beneath the ground, in the catacombs of the Lower Wards.

The entire capital is a marketplace of ideas and discoveries, a melting pot of cultures, tribes, and species who come not just to live, but to exchange goods, ideas, and traditions.

Nobody in Eternos except King Randor knows that the mighty He-Man is actually their lost Prince, Adam. More than anything else, King Randor would love for Adam to lay down his sword, and come home to live and rule by his side in the palace.

CASTLE GRAYSKULL

The single most important location on Eternia is Castle Grayskull. Long ago, it was the home of the legendary King Grayskull: the man who created the Sword of Power, and the first Master of the Universe.

Castle Grayskull is an ancient skull-faced fortress. Outfitted with giant energy cannons and glowing with mystic light, the entire castle hovers in midair. Enter (if you dare) through the toothy Jawbridge, crossing over a bottomless pit!

Adam and Teela wonder if the castle may actually be the bones of a long-gone giant. Krass thinks King Grayskull probably built it to look so spooky that no one would come near it. Duncan says it feels like a ship, and the Supreme Power Chamber is its engine. Whatever the castle is and wherever it came from is a total mystery. Eldress knows the truth, but will not say it . . . yet! Not until her young Masters are ready to know *everything*.

One way or another, Castle Grayskull is clearly not meant for visitors; it's meant to safeguard the greatest power in the universe . . .

The Power of Grayskull is the nexus of all the ancient powers of the universe. It's what gives the weapons of the Masters their charge, and it's located deep within the castle in a chamber known as . . .

THE SUPREME POWER CHAMBER

The Power of Grayskull flows up through the center of this room in a giant column of crackling golden energy. This is where Adam first charged his Power Sword and shared the Power of Grayskull with his friends!

The chamber itself is stately and circular with walls that soar upward until they disappear in mists. There are many doors leading out of the chamber—some may open into other worlds, maybe even other realities. But most of the doors are locked and purposefully so . . . Adam and his friends have tried all the keys, but with no luck!

But if they follow the Power of Grayskull up through the mists above, they enter the Upper Chamber, where the entire cosmos stretches over their heads, and they can see the Power radiating out into the universe all around them.

HOME, SWEET GRAYSKULL

Adam and his allies turn the spooky, gloomy Castle Grayskull into a clubhouse of sorts, a home base to train and plan their next moves against Skeletor!

On the one hand, Castle Grayskull is a perfect choice for a secret headquarters. It's a castle full of secrets. A labyrinth. A spooky puzzle box of magic and mystery. Even its rooms have rooms. On the other hand—*it's a castle full of secrets!*

One time, Duncan prepared a midnight snack in Kitchen Grayskull—and the snack ate him! Adam once flicked on what he thought was a light switch and wound up momentarily turning off all the stars in the galaxy! And they're still looking for the bathroom.

But hey, it's still their home. They may come from different lands, but these rookie warriors are slowly becoming more than just a team. They're becoming . . . a family! And in these halls of mystery, they

train. As they learn to master their weapons, they empower the unique part of themselves that resonates with the universe, turning it into a superpower. They get stronger! And STRONGER! Becoming Masters of their powers . . . *Masters of the Universe!*

They happily explore the Laboratories and the Archive of Forbidden Knowledge in the castle. The Hallway of Holograms and Illusions is a good place to throw a party. There are trapdoors, training rooms, mystic mirrors, and only one bathroom (good luck finding it!). Eldress acts as a den mother of sorts, sometimes providing gentle advice, sometimes cautioning the team not to break things.

The castle is hidden among the highest mountains of Eternia, concealed in layers of magic, and only He-Man's Sword of Power can lift that magic to reveal the castle and lower its Jawbridge. But that's not the only way the castle hides itself. In emergency situations, the castle can magically relocate—but so far only Eldress is able to pull off that trick. The castle also has all kinds of energy turrets and techno-traps along its perimeter as backup defenses.

Adam and the Masters will do whatever it takes to keep the castle safe. If evil reaches the Power of Grayskull inside, it could mean the end of everything, everywhere.

THE TIGER TRIBAL LANDS

The Tiger Tribe village is located in the jungle regions of Eternia. Displaced people and tigers live there together in peace. The Tiger Tribe distrusts both magic and technology and prefers to live a simple life, migrating across the jungle for generations. They have settled recently in huts under the shade of

the crashed airship that brought young Krass into the tribe. All Stripes—people and Tigers in the tribe—live in harmony within their jungle but can never let their guard down. Beastopoid Rqazz and his evil Poacher Bots are a constant threat to the tribe.

AVION

The skylands above Eternia are home to the winged people of Avion and their leader, King Stratos.

Avion is a glistening city carved from elemental rocks that float miles up in the sky. With wings that protrude naturally from their forearms, the Avions soar through the air of their realm: racing to far-flung floating islands, sailing on shimmering air currents, and wheeling through glistening cloud waterfalls.

Stratos and his people love their home. As they say on Avion, *et voilà!* They pride themselves on being above it all. But the menace of Skeletor may change all that.

THE MYSTIC MOUNTAINS

These beautiful lush mountains are covered in thick forests and steeped in magic. Mists cloak the landscape in mystery, for magic grows naturally here—it's in the very soil, and from there it grows in all forms: crystallized in the deepest caves, blooming in exotic flowers, fished from colorful streams.

Legend has it that all sorts of magical relics are hidden here. But along with that treasure, the Mystic Mountains are also home to the webs of the spiderlike fighting warriors known as the Arachna.

LEVIATHAE

The kingdom of Leviathae lies in the very blackest depths of the ocean, where absolutely no light penetrates. There live the Mer-Folk and their ruler, Mer-Man, the king of the high seas.

Long ago, Leviathae was King Grayskull's greatest ally in his war against the Snake Men Empire. But since that time, communication between Leviathae and the rest of Eternia has gone icy cold, and no one has heard from the Mer-Folk in a thousand years.

THE BADLANDS

ternia is a beautiful world, but there are areas so terrifying that you dare not risk visiting, such as the dangerous regions just beyond the Evergreen Forests, a wasteland Eternians have come to refer to as the Badlands.

The Badlands are a mostly dead, empty landscape. Although this land is under the rule of King Randor, it's mostly lawless. To cross it is to risk encounters with bandits.

Though the Badlands are barren, there are some species who call it their home: Speleans, bat-like humanoids that haunt the caves; the Karikoni, armored, crustaceous beasts; Stonedarians, a people made of rock and stone; and dozens more.

THE FRIGHT ZONE

While many modern Eternians think the Snake Men were only creatures of legend, they were, in fact, real. Led by King Hssss, the Snake Men were a historical race of serpentine warriors that nearly snuffed out all life on Eternia—that is, until King Grayskull stopped them once and for all.

Though they are all long gone, the land from which the Snake Men empire spread still spooks people out. Hence its name: the Fright Zone. A haunted, grim, gray landscape, no one visited the Fright Zone willingly . . . until Skeletor.

SNAKE MOUNTAIN

In the farthest reach of the Fright Zone, Skeletor has found his lair: Snake Mountain.

Built into a dark volcanic mountain peak with a large stone serpent wrapped around it, this fortress was once the temple and palace of King Hssss and his Snake Men Empire. Since that time, the mountain lay empty, until Skeletor moved in!

At the base of King Hssss's throne, Skeletor struck the ground with his staff, injecting the earth with his Havoc to create a pit of sickly green ooze: the Forge of Havoc. Now a waterfall of Havoc-green lava pours out of the stone serpent's mouth to form a lake of Havoc at the foot of the mountain below.

And in the energies of this forge, Skeletor created new Dark Power Weapons to assemble his Dark Masters of the Universe! (That's you, Evil-Lyn, Trap Jaw, and Beast Man.)

Skeletor's Havoc is the dark reflection of the Power of Grayskull, and the weapons he made from its energy harness the ancient dark powers of the universe.

Unchecked, Havoc grows, consuming and corrupting all in its path. The Havoc pouring out of Snake Mountain has seeped into all the nooks and crannies of the Fright Zone, reanimating the skeletal remains of long-gone creatures. These voracious Battle Bones now roam the landscape, awaiting Skeletor's command.

THE WIND RAIDER

The heroic Masters of the Universe soar into battle aboard the Wind Raider—a mobile command center and team transport disguised inside an aircraft built for speed.

The ship originally belonged to Kronis, back when he was the man-at-arms for Eternos. When he betrayed King Randor in Prince Keldor's coup, Randor ordered Kronis to be arrested. Kronis escaped in the Wind Raider, and continued using it in his new life of crime. That is, until it became Duncan's escape vehicle, the day he ended his apprenticeship with Kronis to join up with Adam and his friends.

Now, as Man-At-Arms of Castle Grayskull, Duncan has tinkered with the Wind Raider, customizing it for the Masters, and souping it up with a new Grayskull Battle Mode. With the flick of a switch, defensive forcefields engage, and a full array of formidable Grayskull weaponry are at the ready to destroy the evil forces of Skeletor.

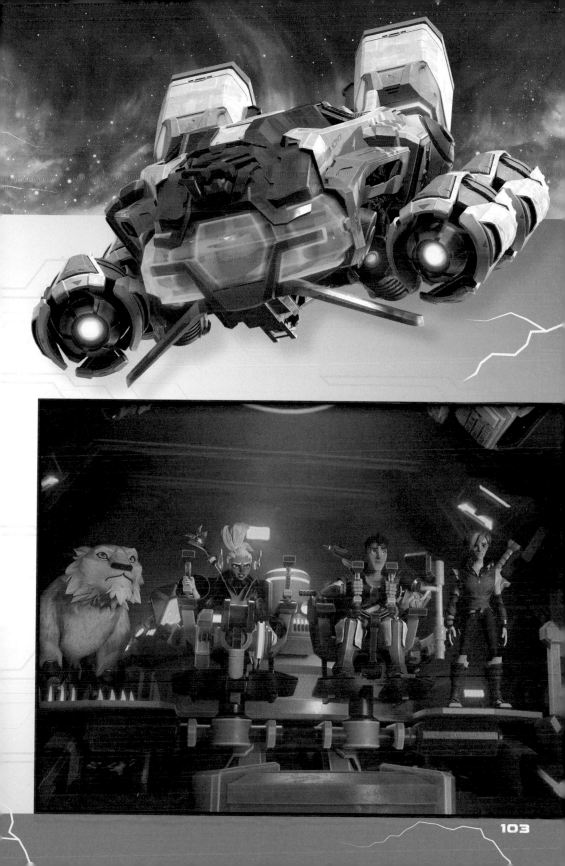

BEASTOPOID CAGE SHIPS

The Beastopoids are a jungle race of savage beast-human hybrids, fierce rivals of the Tiger Tribe. And no Beastopoid is worse than Rqazz the hunter (also known as Beast Man). Cracking his whip, Rqazz launches his Poacher Bots into the wilds to herd his prey into Beastopoid Cage Ships full of captive creatures of the jungle. Their destination: to battle against one another for Rqazz's amusement in his terrible fighting pits.

ETERNIAN ROYAL GUARD VEHICLES

One of the chief responsibilities of King Randor is to keep the people of Eternia safe. But to keep the world safe, you've gotta be able to get there on time! His Royal Guards are equipped with the most advanced airships known to Eternian science, from SKY SLEDS— single-manned hovercrafts that can reach the stratosphere, to ROYAL TRANSPORTS—able to deploy legions of Royal Guardspeople to areas in need.

ROTONS

Though Skeletor recognizes the might of Randor's troops and fleets, he can't say he's a fan of their style. The first thing he'll do when he takes Eternos? Order Trap Jaw to get to work on some new weapons of war. He can't wait to show Eternia how *Skeletor's* Eternos truly rolls!

Trap Jaw knows just the thing to invent: Rotons, hovercrafts encircled by rings of swirling blades that create a vortex of air, ripping the Rotons across land or screeching into the sky to wreak havoc. He's sure Skeletor will be pleased!

A STROKE OF HAVOC

The impossible has happened! Though He-Man and the Masters of the Universe have fought to keep Eternia safe, Skeletor and his Dark Masters have gained the upper hand!

Using his Havoc Staff to control the minds of the Red Legion soldiers, Skeletor and his Dark Masters conquer Eternos with Randor's own army. Now Skeletor sits on the throne!

With Eternos in his bony grip, the Dark Master of Havoc turns his full attention to destroying Castle Grayskull, the source of He-Man and the Masters' power, once and for all!

Can our heroes escape such a fate? Can they destroy the Havoc Staff— breaking Skeletor's grip on the Red Legion, his Dark Masters, and free Eternia? Adam is determined to find out.

THE BATTLE RAGES

It's a lot of pressure to put on the shoulders of a sixteen-year-old boy who never wanted any responsibility to begin with. He's just a regular kid and certainly never dreamed he was a prince.

But inside, Adam has the heart of a champion: He wants to help others, and he's got the courage to stand up to bullies. And now he's got the power to make a difference, as HE-MAN: Master of Power!

Even better, he's not alone, with RAM MA'AM: Master of Demolition! MAN-AT-ARMS: Master of Technology! BATTLE CAT: Master of the Wild! SORCERESS: Master of Magic!

Together, they are HE-MAN and the MASTERS OF THE UNIVERSE!

These five brave friends are ready to save the day.

THEY HAVE THE POWER . . .

. . . AND SO DO YOU.

WILL YOU JOIN THE FIGHT?

It's Master vs. Dark Master! He-Man vs. Skeletor! Fighting for control of Eternia, Castle Grayskull, and ultimate power! In the end, winner takes all!

WHO WILL BECOME THE ULTIMATE MASTER OF THE UNIVERSE?